CURLING
CRUNCH

BY **JAKE MADDOX**

text by Emma Carlson Berne

illustrated by Katie Wood

STONE ARCH BOOKS
a capstone imprint

Published by Stone Arch Books, an imprint of Capstone
1710 Roe Crest Drive, North Mankato, Minnesota 56003
capstonepub.com

Library of Congress Cataloging-in-Publication Data
is available on the Library of Congress website.
ISBN: 9781669007050 (hardcover)
ISBN: 9781669007012 (paperback)
ISBN: 9781669007029 (ebook PDF)

Summary: Maisie loves pitching for her softball team in Arizona,
so she's crushed when she has to move to Minnesota to live with
her dad. Upset about the move and her parents' divorce, Maisie isn't
thrilled when her dad asks her to join his curling team. She thinks
it's a strange sport. But as she learns more about curling—and how
much her dad loves it—she begins to have a change of heart.
When it's crunch time for the team, will Maisie
be able to take charge and lead?

Designer: Sarah Bennett

Consultant: Tim Solie

TABLE OF CONTENTS

CHAPTER ONE

BALLPLAYER

The softball fit perfectly in Maisie's hand. It always did. The feeling of the leather and laces against her palm was the best feeling in the world.

Maisie smacked the ball into her glove and eyed the batter. The girl looked nervous.

She should, Maisie thought.

Maisie breathed deeply, just like she always did before a pitch. *Just one more strike, and then we'll be up to bat*, she thought to herself. She swung her arm for the windup.

Her muscles felt strong. When the ball left her hand, she could tell it would be a strike. There's just something about that magic when all the parts fit together for a perfect pitch.

The batter swung and missed.

"Strike!" the ump called.

"Yeah, girl!" June shouted as she ran over from second base. Maisie gave her best friend a high five and jogged to the dugout.

"Excellent pitching, Maisie," Coach Klein said, looking up from her clipboard. "You're batting first."

Maisie nodded, gulping down water from her bottle.

"Maisie! Maisie! Maisie!" the Flames chanted as she slipped on her batting helmet and swung the bat a few times.

She grinned as she stepped up to the plate.

The ball sped toward her, almost too fast to see. She did what she always does. She let her mind go black and her muscles take over. *Crack!* It was the best sound on Earth.

Maisie stood, watching the ball soar over the outfield fence. As the Flames cheered, she ran the bases for the home run.

The score was 5–3, with the Flames in the lead, of course. They were the top team in their league so far, but the other team was pretty good. They just had to pull off this win to make it to the championship game.

By the seventh inning, the score was tied 8–8. The Flames were batting last, and Sarah was up to bat. Her teammates watched eagerly as she stepped up to the plate. She looked determined. On the first pitch, she smacked the ball out of the field.

"And that'll put us in the championship game," Coach said as Sarah rounded home to end the game.

"Yeah!" Everyone cheered and started slapping hands.

"The championship game will be in three weeks," Coach shouted over the noise. "We'll be playing the Lions."

The girls barely heard her. June was dancing on the dugout bench. Elise and Lucy were holding hands, jumping up and down, and screaming "Champions! Champions!"

Maisie watched her joyous teammates for a moment. Then she slowly walked over to the backstop fence. She pretended she was taking her bag down. She just didn't want anyone to see the tears filling her eyes.

Then someone put a soft hand on her back. Maisie turned around. June was standing there. Tears were running down her face too.

"I can't believe it's your last game," June said. She swiped at her face.

Tears were dripping off Maisie's chin now. "I don't want it to be. I want to stay."

The others began to crowd around.

"Maisie, you'll miss the championship game," Elise moaned. "I can't pitch that game! It has to be you!"

A car honked in the parking lot. Maisie looked over. "My mom's here," she said in almost a whisper. She couldn't talk louder. She was too choked up. "Bye. I love you all. Bye."

Maisie turned and grabbed her bag. She couldn't look back. She didn't want to see her Flames standing there, pressed against the backstop fence, all of them saying goodbye—forever.

CHAPTER TWO

GOODBYE, ARIZONA

"How were the goodbyes?" asked Mom as Maisie got in the car and slammed the door shut. Maisie stared straight ahead.

"Awful. How did you think they'd be?" Maisie said.

Mom was quiet a moment. "I thought they'd be awful. I'm so sorry you have to leave the team, honey."

"Leave the team?" Maisie raised her voice. "Yeah! How about my house, my friends, and everything I've ever known?"

She scrunched her hands into her softball pants, squeezing the fabric. "All because you and Dad can't make it work!" She was shouting now—she knew it. But she couldn't keep it in another minute.

A silence hung in the car for what felt like forever. Mom signaled and pulled into their driveway. She turned off the ignition and sighed.

"A divorce is about more than 'not making it work.' You know that. Dad and I had to end our marriage for a lot of reasons. He worked a lot. I felt like he wasn't around when we needed him. He thinks the move to Minnesota is for the best. I think he's right. It'll be good for us all. It'll give us all a new start."

"It won't be good for me!" Maisie said as she grabbed her bag and got out of the car.

She slammed the door behind her. "The last thing in the world I want is to move to the middle of nowhere. And you're making me!" She ran toward the house.

"Maisie!" Mom called after her. "This is our agreement! Summers here, school year with Dad. We've talked about this! I know it's hard to move in the middle of the school year, but your dad's settled in and ready for you to come now."

Up in her room, Maisie dropped her bag on the rug and got changed. She stared into the mirror on the back of her closet door.

Last year, when Mom and Dad first told her they were getting divorced, she thought it would be like the other divorces she knew about. Dad would get a condo nearby, and she would go there on the weekends. But Dad got a job at a college in Minnesota.

Then Mom and Dad dropped the bombshell. Maisie would be moving out there too, every school year. It was part of their custody agreement.

Well, it's not part of my agreement, Maisie thought, staring at her swollen eyes and blotchy face in the mirror. *I didn't agree to any of this.*

She dumped her bag out onto the bed and pulled out her phone. Quickly, she typed out a text to June.

I swear, they can make me go, but they can't make me stay.

Three gray bubbles, then June's reply popped up. *Whoa, what?*

I mean it. I'm not going to let them do this to me. Maisie pressed the buttons so hard she could feel her fingertips mashing against them. Then rage overwhelmed her.

She threw her phone across the room
as hard as she could. It hit the wall and
tumbled to the floor.

Maisie stood for a time, panting.
Then she picked up her phone. A long
crack in the screen ran from top to bottom.
Broken. Just like her heart.

CHAPTER THREE

HELLO, MINNESOTA

Gray, flat fields spread out below
the plane. Maisie pressed her forehead
to the little plastic window. White snow.
More white snow. Flatness. More flatness.
Was there anything in Minnesota besides
flatness? Well, snow. There was snow.

The plane bumped and sped down
the runway. When the door finally opened,
Maisie tugged her bag from the overhead
bin. She tried to avoid tearing the huge
ticket that hung from her neck on a string.
"Unaccompanied Minor," it read.

Dad was waiting at the end of the jet bridge, holding a huge sign that read, "Welcome to Minnesota, Maisie!" She wanted to fling herself into his arms at the sight of his familiar crinkly eyes and old flannel shirt. Then she remembered she was mad at him and made herself stand back.

"Maize!" He tried to hug her, but she just stood stiffly.

"Hello," she said.

"Ah, okay, I get it." Dad picked up her bag. "No problem. This is a big adjustment. You know what? Let's make a stop on the way home."

"Wherever we're going isn't my home," Maisie muttered. "My home is Phoenix."

"What did you say?" Dad was trying to navigate a crowded moving sidewalk.

"Nothing," Maisie muttered.

Outside the terminal, the cold air hit her like a sledgehammer. The wind pierced her jacket as if it were made of paper. She stuffed her hands deep into her pockets and scrunched down inside her clothes.

"We're going to have to get you a real winter coat and some boots, now that you're a Minnesotan."

Maisie eyed the down parka and woolly boots of a girl heading into the parking garage. She wasn't a Minnesotan. But right now, she wouldn't mind dressing like one.

The car ride was silent. Maisie gazed out the window at the flat fields and warehouses covered with snow. She might as well have been on the moon—Arizona felt so far away. Then Dad pulled up in front of a huge building with a small sign above the door.

"Albans Youth Curling Club," it read.

Maisie sat up. "What are we doing here?"

Dad had a huge grin on his face. "Ah, well, I just wanted to show you something." He got out of the car and opened Maisie's door with a grand sweep of his arm. "This is what I've been doing when I'm not working."

Maisie followed him into a big lobby. "To the Ice," read a sign in front of them. Dad pushed the doors open.

Inside was a huge space that looked something like an ice-skating rink, but the ice was marked with red and blue circles at one end. Some kind of red Astroturf-looking stuff ran down the middle of the rink in a wide strip. Girls about Maisie's age were scattered at one end, some talking and some holding sticks that looked like the dust mop Maisie's mom used at home.

As Maisie watched, one of the girls ran forward in a crouch, pushing a huge stone with a plastic handle attached to the top. She held the dust mop thing in her other hand. The girl shoved the stone forward, and it slid along the ice. Then she ran forward and started doing something with the dust mop. Maisie squinted. The girl was shoving the dust mop thing around in front of the stone really fast, like she was trying to erase the ice with it. The stone slid into the blue circle. Everyone cheered.

Maisie looked up at Dad. "I'm so confused. What's going on?"

CHAPTER FOUR

THE ALBANS YOUTH CURLING CLUB

Dad swept his arm around the arena very dramatically. "This is curling, honey. And this is my side project—the Albans Youth Curling Club! I've always been interested in curling. It's a big deal up here, so I've gotten into it more since I moved. I even decided to coach this girls' team. What do you think?"

Maisie watched another player run forward with the stone. "Harder, harder!" a tall girl with a ponytail yelled as the stone slid forward toward the red and blue circles.

"I think it's bizarre," Maisie said. "What the heck are they doing?"

"They're trying to get the stone into the red circle, which is called the button. When you play a game, you want to get your team's stones closer to the center of the button—the tee—than your opponents' stones. That's how you earn points. But the stones have to be inside that big, blue circle that surrounds the button—the house—to earn a point. The broom is for taking away the friction between the ice and the stone, so it can slide farther." Dad grabbed a broom leaning beside them. "Want to try?"

"No." Maisie turned her back and plopped down on a nearby bench. She pulled out her phone and started texting June.

"Alright." Dad put the broom back.

"Well, I'll just give the team a few instructions, and then we'll go out for dinner. How does that sound?"

"Peachy," Maisie said, but kept her eyes on her phone on purpose. She was being so mean to Dad—she knew.

Help! I'm in the twilight zone, she typed. *These people are totally weird. They're sweeping the ice!*

What the what?! June responded immediately.

I know. It's so stupid, Maisie typed.

Half an hour later, Dad and Maisie sat across from each other in a padded booth at a restaurant called Frank's Diner. Plates with burgers and fries sat in front of them. The food smelled fantastic. Maisie wanted to continue her program of sullenness, but she couldn't resist taking an enormous bite.

"So, I have a proposal, Maizel," Dad said. He squirted ketchup on his fries.

"Could you not call me that?" Maisie kept her eyes on her burger. "Thanks."

Dad paused. "Ah, sure. Anyway, here's my proposal. Our Albans team is doing great, but we're short one player. How about it, honey?"

Maisie took a minute to realize what he was asking. "Dad, no," she said. "Just—no."

But he kept talking. "I thought it would give you something to do while you're up here, until school starts after winter break. And we can work on the game together. I've missed you these last months, Maze."

Maisie was slowly and steadily shaking her head. "No. No. No way am I joining your curling team, Dad!"

"I need you, honey," Dad pleaded. "One of our players, Tess, had to quit because of school. Unless we can come up with one more player, we'll have to forfeit the season."

"No!" Maisie scowled at her burger.

Dad was silent for a while. "Alright. I'll make you a deal, then. Give it a chance. Play with the team through our first game. It'll fall at the end of winter break. If you can do that, I'll buy you a plane ticket back to Arizona so you can see the Flames play in the championship game. Deal?"

Maisie sat still. A plane ticket home. She'd be with her Flames again. Sun, the blue, blue sky, the familiar sandy stones of the desert. She'd be home. A smile spread across her face.

"Deal," she said.

* * *

Back at Dad's, perched on an unfamiliar bed, Maisie pulled out her phone. *Guess what, Dad's buying me plane tix home to see the championship!* she typed to June.

Three dots. Then, *OMG, yay!!!*

Maisie paused. Then she typed the thought that had been in her mind since Dad's proposal. *But . . . here's the thing. I'm only gonna be using it one way.*

Wait, what? June responded.

Yeah, Maisie typed. *Dad doesn't know, but I'm not coming back here. I'm going to stay in AZ for good.*

CHAPTER FIVE

A BIG KICK

"This place feels like a refrigerator," Maisie complained as she and Dad stepped onto the rink the next morning. Today was her first official day as an Albans curler. She tried to ignore the flutters in her stomach as she walked slowly toward the other girls clustered at one end of the ice.

"Team, please welcome our newest player—my daughter Maisie," Dad said. "You may have met her yesterday. Today, she's one of you. I know you'll teach her everything she needs to know about curling."

Which is nothing, Maisie thought as she slung her bag on the bench beside piles of other gear.

"Hi!" a tall girl with her hair pulled back in a puff said. "I'm Bertie, the skip."

"That's the captain," another girl said. She must have seen the look of confusion on Maisie's face. "I'm Ada. Don't worry, we'll explain it all."

Ten minutes later, Maisie found herself standing at one end of the ice rink wearing track pants, a zip-up team jacket, and the weirdest pair of shoes she had ever seen. They were like sneakers, except one had a hard plastic sole that kept slipping around on the ice and the other had a rubber sole with grippers. She was also wearing gloves—and a grumpy scowl. She tried to control the scowl, but it kept coming back.

Bertie, Ada, and the others were doing a good job ignoring it, though.

"Okay, you're going to just slide the stone toward the end," Bertie told her. She pointed to a big, shiny, round stone with a handle on the top. "You want to really shove it."

I cannot believe I'm doing this, Maisie thought as she grimly grasped the handle. She gave a half-hearted shove. The stone moved about a foot and stopped.

Ada giggled. "You have to push it hard!" she called. "Use your muscles!"

Maisie gritted her teeth. *They want hard? I'll shove it hard.* Letting out a grunt, she pushed the stone as hard as she could.

"Whoa!" Bertie called. They all stood and watched as the stone shot across the ice and bounced off a board at the end of the rink.

"Not that hard, Maize," Dad said from the sidelines.

Bertie handed her the dust-mop-looking thing. "You want to try sweeping? You rub it onto the ice in front of the stone. See, the ice is all nubbly. The broom rubs away the rough part of the ice, and the stone can slide farther on the smoother ice."

Maisie nodded. She didn't trust her voice to say another word. She'd scream. What was she doing here? Why was she playing this insane sport? If you could even call it a sport. Sweeping?

She positioned herself near the end of the ice rink like Bertie showed her, and a girl with a high ponytail shoved the stone toward her.

"Now sweep!" Bertie called. "In front of the stone!"

Furiously, Maisie started rubbing the broom back and forth in front of the giant stone, which was sliding slowly down the ice.

"Harder!" Dad called. "Sweep faster!"

Maisie rubbed faster. The stone bumped into her broom. The broom clattered out of her hand.

"Arrggh!" All the frustration that had been building inside her spilled out, and she kicked the stone as hard as she could.

Pain exploded through her big toe and traveled up her leg. She fell to the ice, clutching her foot. "Ooohh," she moaned.

Dad and Bertie rushed over to her, with the others behind them. Maisie looked up at their worried faces. Her foot was throbbing.

"That was silly," Dad said as he helped her to her feet.

"I know," Maisie mumbled. Silly or not, she knew one thing for sure—she wouldn't be rubbing that stupid broom on the ice tomorrow—or the next day, for that matter.

CHAPTER SIX

ALL CURLING

Maisie's toe throbbed. She'd been resting all day in Dad's recliner with her foot propped up on a pillow, but it still hurt. Toward the end of the afternoon, Dad staggered into the living room with a big storage box.

"Whew!" he said, putting the box down on the coffee table. "I found some old stones in the storage room at the rink. You want to help me clean them?"

That was the last thing she wanted, but considering she'd been staring out the window all afternoon, she couldn't exactly say she was busy. "Yeah, sure, whatever."

She swung her leg carefully off the recliner. Dad pulled the stones out of the box and lined them up on the coffee table.

"Might as well watch something while we work." He picked up the remote and clicked through until he landed on a curling channel Maisie had never seen before.

"Dad!" she protested.

He looked sheepish and mischievous. "It's got great highlights from the last Olympics!" He handed her a wet rag. "Just get the dirt off, okay?"

Maisie rubbed a stone until the rag turned black. She held up the rag and made a face. "Yuck."

"That's a lot of dirt!" Dad said. "Okay, wait. Look." He paused the TV. "Watch how this player is pushing the stone. She has to get her eyes close to the ice, but still keep her back straight. It's harder than it looks."

Dad's face was all lit up. Maisie hadn't seen him like that in a long time.

"Look! It was a freeze!" Dad pointed.

"What? What was it?" In spite of herself, Maisie found she was leaning forward.

Dad slo-moed the action on the screen. "Okay, this is a really hard shot. She sends the stone down the ice."

Maisie watched the stone slide as if it were moving on its own. It was strangely hypnotic.

"Then the sweeper brushes the ice ahead of it, but just the right amount," Dad said.

"Now look! The stone came up right behind the other team's stone. It rests just behind it, like they've been frozen together. That makes it harder for the other team to knock it out of the house. It's a really rare move— and probably my favorite."

It was kind of cool, Maisie had to admit. You had to be really careful and precise. "Kind of like in softball," she said aloud.

"What, hon?" Dad picked up another stone and started rubbing it with the rag.

"Oh. Nothing," Maisie replied. "I just was thinking that you have to line the stones up exactly right, and if you mess up even a little, you'll miss—like batting in softball. You have to gauge when to swing at just the right moment, or you'll get a strike."

"Right." Dad scrubbed a black spot. "And if you mess up a lot, you'll miss entirely.

Kind of like me with the divorce."

Maisie tried not look at Dad. She didn't really want to hear about their divorce today.

"I know I've missed out on a lot of things in your life, Maize. I was gone a lot. But I want that to change. I want us to have things we do together. I was hoping curling might be one of them."

"But Dad, curling is your thing," Maisie said. "Not mine. Mine was softball, and you and Mom made me leave it behind."

Dad smiled as if he'd been waiting for this moment. He dug into his back pocket and pulled out a folded piece of paper. "You haven't left it behind forever." He handed her the paper.

Maisie unfolded it. It was a printout of a round-trip ticket to Phoenix for one week from now—the date of the championship.

"Dad, thank you!" She hugged him, squeezing the paper. "But I thought you weren't buying the ticket until after I played in a game."

"I figured you needed a pick-me-up after yesterday's practice," Dad said. "But I'm holding you to our deal—so take care of that toe."

"Yeah, I will," replied Maisie. "I'm sorry I was so awful at practice yesterday."

"It's okay," Dad said. "I think you're paying for it with that toe right now."

"It feels better," she said, picking up her rag. "Let's finish these. But no more Olympic highlights, okay?"

"Okay," Dad agreed, laughing.

CHAPTER SEVEN

NIGHTTIME ICE

Maisie somehow felt lighter at practice the next day. Her toe barely hurt at all, and she was surprised to hear herself laughing with Ada when her stone flew right off the ice.

Maisie was sweeping hard after a throw when she heard Bertie nearby. "Yeah, the pond at eight tonight?" Bertie said.

"Maisie, you want to come?" Bertie called over. "We're going to do some old-school curling tonight on Ada's family's pond."

"Yeah, come!" Ada chimed in. "It's so fun."

"Um, sure," Maisie said uncertainly. She didn't know what she was signing up for, but it would definitely beat sitting at home with Dad another night and watching Olympic highlights.

* * *

The pond was glowing blue and green and white that night when Dad dropped her off near a clearing in the woods. The others were already there, pushing the stones back and forth on the frozen pond. Maisie stood for a moment, watching them.

Huge, dark pines circled the clearing, like guards watching over the ice. Blobby snow crusted their branches and covered the ground, muffling the girls' shrieks and the scrape of the stones sliding across the ice.

The frozen ice glowed under the moonlight, almost as if it were lit from within. Maisie had never seen anything like it.

"Maisie!" Bertie, bundled up in a big parka, waved. "Get ready! This one's for you!"

Maisie stepped onto the frozen pond just as Bertie crouched and slid a stone toward her—fast. Before she could think, Ada thrust a broom into her hand. Maisie started sweeping, skipping out of the way of the heavy stone, until it bumped into a fallen branch and came to rest.

"Clean!" Bertie yelled.

"The branch is the button," someone else explained to Maisie.

"This is awesome," Maisie said, looking around. "Do you do this a lot?"

"Yeah, sometimes," Ada said. "Dad blows the snow off and tests the ice to make sure it's thick enough. He said it was twenty-four inches thick today!"

"Nice!" Maisie said. Then she had an idea. "Bertie, stone race!" she called. She ran to the end of the pond and slid to a stop. "Here's the finish line!" She waved her arms.

"Oh, you're all going down," Bertie called back. The others scrambled into line. Laughing, one by one they sent the stones gliding down the ice toward Maisie.

"Now, sweep!" Ada yelled and ran forward. Everyone else did too, at the same time, until Bertie tripped on her stone. Then another girl fell on her, and Ada went down too. As she did, she reached out and yanked Maisie down.

Maisie collapsed onto the heap, laughing.

As she lay on her back on the ice, gazing up at the brilliant moon, she thought that this was the first time since leaving Phoenix that she'd felt perfectly, simply happy.

* * *

Back at home, Maisie flopped on her bed. Just then, her phone lit up with a video call from June.

"Hey!" her best friend said as her face came onto the screen.

"Hi!" Maisie held the phone up over her head. "I'm sooo tired. We were out on this pond tonight."

"Who's 'we'?"

"Just my team. Goofing around."

"Not your team," June said. "The Flames are your team, right?"

"Oh yeah, of course!" Maisie responded.

She dug into the drawer on her nightstand and pulled out the ticket printout Dad had given her and held it up to the screen. "Look!"

"Ooh! OMG, I can't wait for you to be back!" June said. "You're still doing your plan, right?"

"Yeah, of course." Maisie felt an odd sensation in her stomach as she spoke—a sinking feeling. She felt confused, thinking about getting on the plane to Arizona and not coming back—lying to Dad.

She and June chatted a few minutes more and hung up. Maisie brushed her teeth and climbed into bed. She stared at the ceiling. Just a couple of days ago, she knew exactly what she wanted. Now, she was all mixed up inside. And how was she going to get sorted out?

CHAPTER EIGHT

WE'RE NOT FORFEITING!

"Are you nervous?" Bertie asked two days later. Their first game was starting in ten minutes. Maisie breathed deeply and focused on fixing the laces on her curling shoes.

"Yeah," she said finally. "But I'm ready."

"Brooms up!" Bertie called. The team clicked their brooms together.

"Albans!" they shouted and scattered to take their places at the end of the sheet. The pebbly ice stretched out in front of them, ready for throwing. The other team was already there, wearing red.

"Alright, team!" Dad called from the sidelines. "Feet solid, eyes on the button. Maisie, don't throw too hard. Ada, put muscle into your sweeping."

Maisie nodded, trying to ignore her heart pounding in her chest. She was throwing first.

She stepped up to the sheet. "Come on, Maisie!" she heard someone behind her yell. She grasped the red handle of the stone and narrowed her eyes, crouching low and aiming it at the red button at the other end. She pushed. Then Ada ran forward with her broom to sweep.

"Harder!" Bertie yelled.

The stone slid forward as if pulled on an invisible string. It slid closer to the blue circle, then the red.

"Yeah, Maisie!" Dad shouted, coming forward. Then Maisie saw him stumble, trip, and smack his face into the low metal barrier that separated the rink from the sidelines.

Everyone in the rink gasped. Dad lifted his head, his hand over his face and blood pouring from his nose. The referee whistled for a time-out and the Albans ran to Dad on the bench.

"Yourb doing greap!" he said to them through the blood.

Ada's mom, who was a doctor, was already there. She took a look at his nose.

"You've got a broken nose," she told him. "You're going to be fine, but you need to go to the ER to get checked out right away."

"Ibe can't," Dad said through the blood. "We're in the middle of the game!"

Ada's mom was already moving him toward the exit. "Sorry, girls," she yelled back over her shoulder. "I'll call Ada as soon as we get him seen."

As Dad disappeared out the glass doors and murmurs ran through the crowd, the other team's skip spoke up. "That's it, right?" she said. "They'll have to forfeit. They can't play without a coach, right?" she asked the referee.

Maisie stepped forward and said, "We're not forfeiting!" The words came out before she could stop them. But as soon as she spoke, she knew she'd said the right thing.

She turned to Bertie and the others. "Right, Albans? We're not going to forfeit! My dad wouldn't want us to, and we're not going to."

"Yeah!" Bertie said right away. "What she said, ref!"

"Can we check the rules, ref?" the other coach asked.

"Hang on." The referee picked up a handbook hanging from a hook on the wall. He flipped through it. Maisie held her breath. She could feel the rest of the team tensing up too.

Then the referee looked up. "Presence of coaching staff not necessary for game play." He tapped the book. "Says it right here—Rule 14.6." He blew his whistle. "Play resumed."

"Let's do it, Albans!" Maisie shouted. The team crowded around her. "Let's play like my dad would want us to!"

CHAPTER NINE

HOME FOR GOOD

The Albans led all through the first half, with Bertie calling out the throws. Maisie could feel them pulling together, like she used to feel with the Flames when they'd be in the bottom of an inning with the bases loaded. Everyone was throwing carefully and thinking of nothing but the game.

Then it was her turn to throw. It was going to be really tricky. One of the other team's yellow stones was close the center of the button. She needed to get her stone closer to the center to win the round—and the game. And she couldn't risk hitting the other stones nearby and bouncing farther away.

Maisie looked to the sidelines, but Dad wasn't there, of course. Her throat ached suddenly, but she swallowed it back and stepped up to the ice.

"Wait!" Ada called. "My mom's got your dad on video call." She thrust the phone into Maisie's hand. Everyone crowded around behind her. There was Dad on the screen with a huge bandage taped over his nose. He was in the emergency room. Maisie could see the monitors behind him.

"Dad, are you okay?" she asked, squeezing the phone. "We didn't have to forfeit!"

"Because of you," Dad croaked. His voice was hoarse, but his grin was the same. "Ada told her mom how you stood up to the other team. That's my girl!"

"I'm throwing next," Maisie told him. "But the button is really crowded. I don't know—" Then she had an idea. "Dad! Stay on the phone, okay?" She handed the phone to Ada, who held it up so Dad could see.

"Bertie, freeze," she said. Bertie nodded. Maisie grasped the handle of the red stone. She crouched and eyed the ice. Just like in softball, she could feel in her body just how much to push. She cleared her head. She let her muscles take over. The yellow stone gleamed on the ice ahead.

Maisie pushed. The stone glided down the ice. Bertie swept carefully. The team watched and held their breath. Then, it happened. The red stone came to rest just behind the yellow one, barely touching it. The Albans had won the final round—and the game!

"Ahhh!" Maisie screamed. She hugged Bertie and then ran over to Ada, who was still holding up her phone.

"A freeze, Maisie! You did it!" Dad shouted from the phone. "I'm so proud of you!"

Grinning, Maisie took the phone from Ada. "Thanks," she said. "Cool, right?"

"So cool. I'll be home tonight and we'll talk it all over," he said, smiling.

"The doctor's here," a nurse said in the background. Maisie gave Ada her phone.

She couldn't stop smiling either, just
like Dad.

* * *

"Maize!" Dad called from the living room
when Ada's mom dropped Maisie off after
the game. "Get in here and let's discuss your
big move!"

Maisie peeked into the living room.
Dad was sitting in the recliner with his feet
up. His face was still bandaged, but blood
free—thank goodness.

"Yeah, be right in. Just got to do
something quick first," Maisie replied.

Maisie went up to her room. She pulled
open her nightstand drawer. The plane
ticket was there, right on top where she'd left
it after the last time she'd talked to June.

Maisie pulled the ticket out of the drawer.

Then, she sat down on the edge of her bed. She ran her fingers over the print. Quietly, she tore it in half, then in half again. She dropped the pieces into her wastebasket and stood up to go downstairs.

She and Dad had a lot to talk about.

ABOUT THE AUTHOR

 Emma Carlson Berne is the author of many books in the Jake Maddox series, including *Snowboarding Surprise* and *Ice Clash*. She often writes about sports, animals, and Jewish history and culture. Emma lives in Cincinnati, Ohio, with her husband, three boys, one grumpy cat, and one friendly cat.

ABOUT THE ILLUSTRATOR

 Since graduating from Loughborough University School of Art and Design in 2004, Katie Wood has been a freelance illustrator. From her studio in Leicester, England, she creates bright and lively illustrations for books and magazines all over the world.

GLOSSARY

button (BUHT-uhn)—the small circle on the ice that a curler aims for when throwing

custody (KUHS-tuh-dee)—the responsibility to take care of and make decisions for someone

divorce (di-VORSS)—the legal end of a marriage

forfeit (FOR-fuht)—to lose a game because a requirement has not been met

friction (FRIK-shuhn)—a force created when two objects rub together; it slows down objects

hypnotic (hip-NOT-ik)—tending to cause a sleep-like state

minor (MYE-nur)—a person who is under the age of eighteen

nubbly (NUHB-lee)—having small lumps

sheet (SHEET)—the ice on which curling is played

throw (THROH)—the push that moves the stone down the ice

unaccompanied (un-uh-KUHM-puh-need)—alone, without a companion

DISCUSSION QUESTIONS

1. Maisie has to leave her friends, her mom, and the sport she loves, which is really hard for her. Think about a time when you had to say goodbye to someone or had to stop doing something you loved. How did you feel? What did you do to help yourself with that transition?

2. Maisie changes over the course of the story. At first, she wants to go back to Arizona. Gradually, she starts to enjoy being in Minnesota and learning about curling. Look back through the book. At what point do you think Maisie's feelings begin to shift? Provide evidence from the text.

3. At the end of the story, Maisie decides not to go to back to Arizona. Do you agree with her choice? Explain why or why not.

WRITING PROMPTS

1. This story is told from Maisie's point of view. Switch it up and write a letter from June to Maisie, telling her about everything that's been happening in Arizona. How is June's perspective different from Maisie's?

2. Pretend that you are Maisie one year after the end of this book. You have to write an essay for class titled "Why I Love Curling." What will you say? How does playing the sport make you feel?

3. At the end of the book, Maisie decides to stay in Minnesota. Imagine that she makes the opposite decision and decides to go back to Arizona. Write a different ending for the book. Is Maisie happy she decided to go back? Is she regretful?

MORE ABOUT CURLING

The first curling match ever recorded took place in Scotland in 1541. It was a game between a monk and a relative of his boss—the abbot.

Curling stones are made of granite from one of two places—Scotland or Wales. They usually weigh 38 to 44 pounds (17 to 20 kilograms). All of the curling stones used in the Olympics are now made of granite from the tiny, uninhabited Scottish island of Ailsa Craig.

Early curling brooms were . . . actual brooms. They were made of corn straws and had wood handles, just like the brooms people use to sweep their homes.

Curling ice isn't smooth. It's pebbled with tiny ice nubs all over. This helps reduce the friction between the bottom of the stone and the ice itself. If the ice were smooth, the stone would slide too slowly.

Curling became an Olympic sport in 1924 at the first Winter Games in Chamonix, France. Only men were allowed to compete. Great Britain took home the gold that year, but all of the players were from Scotland.